D0295964

A Band of Dirty Pirates

A humorous
rhyming story

First published in 2005 by
Franklin Watts
96 Leonard Street
London
EC2A 4XD

Franklin Watts Australia
45–51 Huntley Street
Alexandria
NSW 2015

Text © Damian Harvey 2005
Illustration © Graham Philpot 2005

A CIP catalogue record for this book is available
from the British Library.

ISBN 0 7496 5941 6 (hbk)
ISBN 0 7496 5947 5 (pbk)

Series Editor: Jackie Hamley
Series Advisors: Dr Barrie Wade, Dr Hilary Minns
Design: Peter Scoulding

Printed in Hong Kong / China

A Band of
Dirty Pirates

Written by
Damian Harvey

Illustrated by
Graham Philpot

W
FRANKLIN WATTS
LONDON•SYDNEY

Damian Harvey
"When I was little I loved stories about the sea and I always wondered what it would be like to be a pirate."

Graham Philpot
"Ahoy there shipmates! For an illustrator, there is no better job than to draw a band of dirty pirates!"

There was once a band of pirates,

Who sailed the seven seas:

A band of dirty pirates,

All with dirty knees.

6

7

They never washed their faces.

They never washed their hands.

Their fingernails were full of muck

From digging in the sands.

Jolly Roger was their captain,

And the dirtiest one of all.

He hadn't had a proper bath
Since he was very small.

After school, one summer's day,

He ran away to sea.

His mum had often wondered
Just where her son could be.

Then one day she saw his ship

Out sailing in the bay.

So she rowed out to say hello
Before it sailed away.

Roger's mum was angry
When she saw the dirty bunch.

She made them walk the plank

For a wash before their lunch.

She made them rub and scrub
Till they were squeaky clean.

29

Now they're the cleanest pirates
That the world has ever seen!

Notes for parents and teachers

READING CORNER has been structured to provide maximum support for new readers. The stories may be used by adults for sharing with young children. Primarily, however, the stories are designed for newly independent readers, whether they are reading these books in bed at night, or in the reading corner at school or in the library.

Starting to read alone can be a daunting prospect. READING CORNER helps by providing visual support and repeating words and phrases, while making reading enjoyable. These books will develop confidence in the new reader, and encourage a love of reading that will last a lifetime!

If you are reading this book with a child, here are a few tips:

1. Make reading fun! Choose a time to read when you and the child are relaxed and have time to share the story.

2. Encourage children to reread the story, and to retell the story in their own words, using the illustrations to remind them what has happened.

3. Give praise! Remember that small mistakes need not always be corrected.

READING CORNER covers three grades of early reading ability, with three levels at each grade. Each level has a certain number of words per story, indicated by the number of bars on the spine of the book, to allow you to choose the right book for a young reader:

GRADE 1	GRADE 2	GRADE 3
50 words	130 words	250 words
70 words	160 words	350 words
100 words	200 words	450 words